SO MANY Sounds

BY
TIM McCANNA

ILLUSTRATED BY
ANDY J. MILLER

ABRAMS APPLESEED
NEW YORK

LISTEN! DO YOU HEAR A SOUND?
NOISES COME FROM ALL AROUND.

SOFT AND GENTLE,
LOUD AND CLEAR, OH
SO MANY SOUNDS
TO HEAR!

TEAPOT WHISTLES.

TOASTER POPS.

BACON SIZZLES.

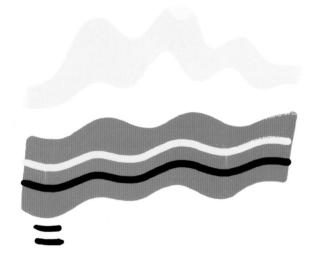

PANCAKE FLOPS.

DISHES **CLATTER**.
FAUCET **DRIPS**.

BUTTONS **SNAP**,

AND ZIPPER **ZIPS**.

CHIPMUNKS **CHITTER.**
SPARROWS **TWEET.**

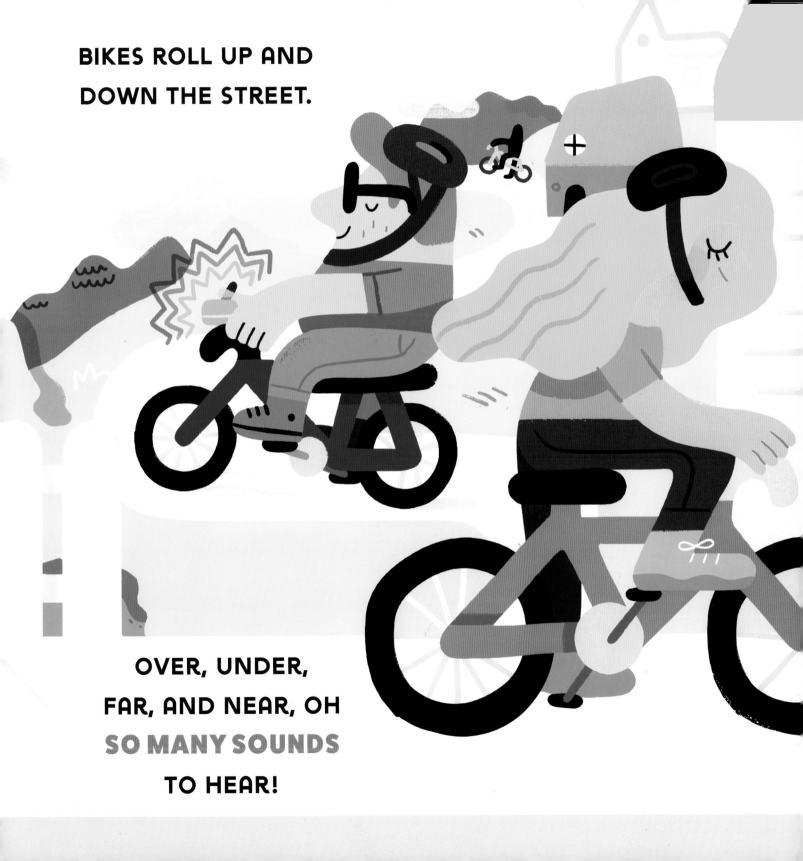

BIKES ROLL UP AND DOWN THE STREET.

OVER, UNDER, FAR, AND NEAR, OH **SO MANY SOUNDS** TO HEAR!

SNEAKERS **STAMP**, AND
CLASSROOMS **BUSTLE**.

PENCILS **SCRATCH**,
AND PAPERS **RUSTLE**.

WHISPERS, GIGGLES, SHOUTS, AND SLURPS.
MUNCHING, CRUNCHING,
GULPS, AND BURPS.

FIELD TRIP TIME!
TODAY'S THE DAY!
HOP ON BOARD—
WE'RE ON OUR WAY!

ALL THE CHILDREN
CLAP AND CHEER. OH
SO MANY SOUNDS
TO HEAR!

FREIGHT TRAINS WHOOSH,

AND AIRPLANES ZOOM.

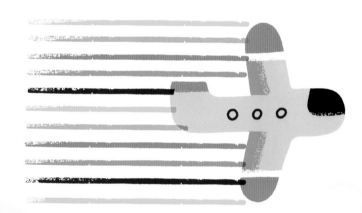

TUGBOATS TOOT, AND

DUMP TRUCKS BOOM.

TAXIS **HONK**,

AND SIRENS **BLAST**.

FIRE ENGINE
ROARING PAST!

DRILL BITS GRIND,
AND HAMMERS BANG.
WORKERS HOLLER.
WRENCHES CLANG.

THROUGH THE TUNNEL, BY THE PIER, OH **SO MANY SOUNDS** TO HEAR!

THUNDER **RUMBLES**.
BREEZES **BLOW**.
WINDOWS **RATTLE**—
TIME TO GO!

SCREEN DOOR OPENS;
HINGES SQUEAK.
HUGS AND KISSES
ON THE CHEEK.

CRICKETS **CHIRP**.
THE CLOCK
STRIKES EIGHT.

SOMEONE **YAWNS**—
IT'S GETTING LATE.

AS THE MOON
AND STARS APPEAR . . .

. . . ONLY QUIET
SOUNDS TO HEAR.

COVERS **RUFFLE**.
"NIGHTY-NIGHT."

CLICK! THE SWITCH
TURNS OFF THE LIGHT.

NO MORE NOISES.
NOT A PEEP.

EVERYONE IS
SOUND ASLEEP.

ZZZZZZZ

LIBRARY OF CONGRESS CONTROL NUMBER: 2017953239
ISBN: 978-1-4197-3156-3

TEXT COPYRIGHT © 2018 TIM MCCANNA
ILLUSTRATIONS COPYRIGHT © 2018 ANDY J. MILLER
BOOK DESIGN BY ALYSSA NASSNER

PRINTED AND BOUND IN CHINA
10 9 8 7 6 5 4 3 2 1

FOR BULK DISCOUNT INQUIRIES,
CONTACT SPECIALSALES@ABRAMSBOOKS.COM.

ABRAMS The Art of Books
195 Broadway, New York, NY 10007
abramsbooks.com